A Beautiful Pearl
Nancy Whitelaw

Illustrated by Judith Friedman

Linda –
It was
wonderful
meeting you
at Highlights.
Good luck on
your writing.
Nancy Whitelaw
July 2006

eio@netsync.net

Albert Whitman & Company, Morton Grove, Illinois

Design by Susan Cohn.
The text of this book is set in Goudy Old Style.

Text © 1991 by Nancy Whitelaw.
Illustrations © 1991 by Judith Friedman.
Published in 1991 by Albert Whitman & Company,
6340 Oakton Street, Morton Grove, Illinois 60053-2723.
Published simultaneously in Canada by General Publishing, Limited, Toronto.
All rights reserved. Printed in U.S.A.
10 9 8 7 6 5 4 3 2 1

Library of Congress Cataloging-in-Publication Data

Whitelaw, Nancy.
    A beautiful pearl / Nancy Whitelaw; pictures by Judith Friedman.
        p.   cm.
    Summary: Although her mind is deteriorating from the effects of Alzheimer's disease,
Grandma presents Lisa with a special gift on her birthday.
    ISBN 0-8075-0599-4
    [1. Alzheimer's disease—Fiction. 2. Grandmothers—Fiction. 3. Birthdays—Fiction.]
I. Friedman, Judith, 1945- ill. II. Title.
PZ7.W5869Be   1991
[Fic]—dc20   90-28761
                                                                    CIP
                                                                    AC

To my mother, my father, and my sister—
they share the pain of Alzheimer's. N.W.

To my mother-in-law, Ethel Mae Nagel. J.F.

All day I wonder if my grandmother will give me the special present for my birthday. Mom waits for me after school, and we drive right to Grandma's.

Mom unlocks the door. Grandma is in the front hall wearing a fur jacket, plaid slacks, and fuzzy red slippers. "Let's get out of here," she says.

My mom takes her arm. "No, Mother, we came to see you because it's Lisa's birthday."

"Okay. We'll go in and wait for Lisa."

"But Grandma, I'm Lisa, and I'm *here*," I say.

She doesn't answer me. She just goes inside and sits down with her jacket on.

Grandma has what they call Alzheimer's disease. That's why sometimes she doesn't know who we are. Sometimes she doesn't know who *she* is, either. Last week, I laughed right out loud when she said that she and I are sisters. Grandma got mad and shook her finger at me. She always does that when she doesn't like what somebody says. "I ought to know my own sister, I guess," she told me.

Now my mom helps Grandma take her jacket off.

"I'll hang it up for you," I say.

"No, no, I'm not sick. I can do it myself." Grandma grabs the jacket from my mom. She stuffs it behind a pillow on the couch. It makes the pillow stick out funny.

Grandma smiles at us. "There, now I'll know where to find it when I want it."

"I brought our album," I say. "Grandma, let's look at it together."

I have to clean off the couch so we can sit down. Scarves and hats and pocketbooks and newspapers are all over the cushions. Grandma likes to take things from one place and put them somewhere else.

I pat the empty place beside me, and Grandma sits down. I love sitting beside her—she's a kid-size grown-up. That's not because she has Alzheimer's; she just stopped growing when she got to be five feet tall. I wonder if I will, too.

I open the album to the picture of me talking to the monkeys at the zoo.

"Remember when you took this picture? You said, 'Lisa, you make a great monkey.' "

Grandma looks at the picture and smiles.

We find the picture of Grandma carrying me when I was real little. And there's one of her holding my birthday bike steady so I can get on it. And here's Grandma and me telling secrets in the kitchen.

"Remember, Grandma? We were whispering about how to get Mom to let me stay up late and watch TV with you. And Mom sneaked up and took our picture."

Mom pokes her head out of the kitchen. "It's almost time for the cake. I'm heating water for tea for us, and I'll get milk for you, Lisa." Mom doesn't know that when I used to stay alone with Grandma, both of us drank tea.

Mom shows Grandma the birthday cake with my name on it.

"Good, I love birthdays. Happy birthday, Lisa," says Grandma.

She holds out her arms to me, and we hug each other. Grandma's skin is really soft. I love to feel it on my cheeks.

"I knew you wouldn't forget me, Grandma," I tell her.

I'm still wondering if Grandma will give me a pearl for my necklace. The day I was born, she gave my mom a pearl to keep for me. Every birthday since then, she's given me another one. When I am twenty years old, I will have a whole beautiful necklace from my grandmother.

Every year when Grandma gives me the special present, she says the same thing. I know it by heart. She says, "To Lisa—a beautiful pearl for a beautiful girl."

My mom didn't tell me, but I bet she got the pearl for Grandma to give to me. Now that Grandma is sick, she can't go shopping anymore. When she needs something, my mom or my Aunt Jane or Mrs. Washburn gets it. Mrs. Washburn is the lady who lives with Grandma and takes care of her.

A while ago, when she wasn't so sick, Grandma went shopping by herself. She went to the grocery store on the corner and bought ten packages of hot dog rolls.

Then she asked the clerk how she could get home. The clerk called the police to help Grandma. A policewoman found her name and address in her pocketbook, and she drove Grandma back. I wish I could have seen my grandma in a squad car!

After that, Mrs. Washburn moved into Grandma's house.

"Lisa, I want to show you something special upstairs," says Grandma.

I know it's my pearl—I *know* it is!

"I'll go too, Mother," says Mom.

Grandma shakes her finger at Mom. "I didn't ask you. I asked this one." She looks at me.

I make a circle with my thumb and finger to tell Mom that I'll be okay with Grandma.

I take Grandma's hand. It's fun to hold hands with somebody just my size but a lot older.

Sometimes, when my grandmother isn't talking funny or acting funny, I make believe that she doesn't have Alzheimer's. I pretend that she's the same grandmother I've always had. Going up the stairs, I remember how we used to ride the escalators in big stores, just for fun—up and down, up and down. After each trip, Grandma would say, "How about one more time, Lisa?"

"Now what do I want?" she asks in a loud voice when we get to the top step. She turns around and glares at me.

I hope Grandma doesn't wake up Mrs. Washburn. She's a nice lady, and she has to take a nap every afternoon because sometimes Grandma keeps her awake at night.

"I think you were going to show me something in your room, Grandma," I say.

"I guess so."

I follow Grandma into her bedroom.

We almost trip on the blankets and sheets and pillows that are all over the floor. There's a big pile of stuff on Grandma's bed—underwear, towels, jewelry boxes, old photographs, earrings, pins, and necklaces. It looks as if somebody tossed things up in the air just to watch them fall on the bed.

My grandmother looks at me. "Now what?" she asks.

"You came up here for something special, remember?"

She doesn't answer. She picks up a gold chain necklace, but it falls on the bed. She picks up one of the jewelry boxes and runs her finger around the bottom. Then she does that again and again. She watches her finger go from corner to corner. I know she's forgotten about the pearl.

Mom comes upstairs. "Let's go downstairs, Mother. It's time for Lisa's cake."

Mom takes the box out of Grandma's hand and puts it on the bed. Then she holds Grandma's arm while they go downstairs. Grandma doesn't say anything.

When we are sitting at the kitchen table, Mom lights the candles on my cake.

"It's chocolate, Grandma. It's real gooey, like the cupcakes you and I used to make."

Grandma doesn't look at the cake. She's staring at a picture on the kitchen wall. It's a photo of our family picnic two years ago. Grandma wasn't sick then. She and I stayed in swimming longer than anybody else.

Right now, Grandma is sitting stiff and straight like a soldier. Her crooked fingers are folded together as if she's praying. Her tiny feet are flat on the floor inside those big red slippers. She just sits, not looking at us, not saying anything.

Mom says, "Let's help Lisa blow out the candles. One . . . two . . . three . . . *blow!*"

Grandma doesn't pay any attention to us, so Mom and I blow out all the candles without her.

"You get your wish," Mom says.

"I wished Grandma would get better."

"For heaven's sakes, Lisa, why did you say that? I'm not sick." Grandma is looking at me now. "It's your mother who is sick. Too bad she can't be here to celebrate your birthday."

"No, Mother, I'm not sick," says Mom. "I'm right here." She smiles, but just her mouth is smiling, not her eyes.

"Well, I'm glad to hear that you're better now," says Grandma. "Let's enjoy this beautiful cake, and then I'll get Lisa's present."

Grandma remembers!

We all like the cake, but probably I like it best. I save the frosting for last. I put a whole gob in my mouth and push it around so every tooth gets some.

After a while, Grandma says, "You'd better go now. Jim will be home any minute, and I have to get supper."

Jim is my grandfather, but he's been dead for a long time.

"Well," my mom says softly, "I guess Dad won't be coming. Mrs. Washburn will eat with you."

"You're wrong," says Grandma. "Jim's coming, and I'm going to cook supper for him."

Mom's eyes are wet and shiny. She doesn't say anything. She stands up and nods her head at me. I know she's telling me to help clear the table.

"Oh, Lisa, you didn't get your present yet," says Grandma. "Let me look for it now."

Grandma looks under our birthday napkins. She goes over to the kitchen counter and stares at the canisters. She opens a drawer and takes out some towels and puts them on the counter. Then she looks at me and frowns.

"It's okay, Grandma. Really it is," I say.

"Lisa's right," says my mother. "We'll look for it some other day. Just let me cut some more cake for you and Mrs. Washburn, and—"

"I'm going to get Lisa's present out of the refrigerator," says my grandmother.

The *refrigerator?* Maybe Mom didn't help her get a pearl for me, after all.

Grandma opens the refrigerator door and takes out a butter dish. She puts it on the table in front of me. Then she takes out a big head of lettuce and puts it in front of Mom. She goes back to the refrigerator.

"Here it is," she says.

She brings out a tiny square box and hands it to me. "It's a beautiful pearl," she says.

My fingers are shaking because I'm scared that maybe Grandma put something different in the box. Maybe it isn't a pearl.

I push up the velvet cover. My present is sitting there, on a dark blue pillow. My shiny white birthday pearl.

"Oh, Grandma, thank you, thank you. It's a beautiful pearl for . . . " In my heart, I beg her to finish it.

"It's a beautiful pearl, a beautiful pearl." Grandma laughs.

"A beautiful pearl for a beautiful girl," I say.
"Yes, Lisa, you're a beautiful girl."
"I love you, Grandma."

A Note about Alzheimer's Disease

Alzheimer's disease is the most common form of dementia, a deterioration in intellectual performance. Some of the symptoms are confusion, loss of memory, disorientation in time and space, personality change, and an inability to maintain personal hygiene.

The cause of this brain disease is not known, and no cure has been found. The number of Alzheimer's victims in the United States was estimated at four million in 1990. Ten percent of people over age sixty-five are affected; over age eighty-five, forty-seven percent are victims.

A youngster who loves a victim of Alzheimer's carries a difficult burden. No one can answer the hard questions: Why did Grandma get Alzheimer's? What makes her forget so much? Why can't the doctors make her better? Yesterday she knew me—why doesn't she know me today? Will I get Alzheimer's?

Adults cannot shield a child from this agony. But they can offer sympathy and love. And often, a child has something to teach grownups. In *A Beautiful Pearl*, Lisa concentrates on the present. She understands that no one has answers to all the questions about Alzheimer's. But she is confident that her grandmother is being taken care of in the best possible way. She and Grandma share a fleeting glance of recognition, a flicker of happiness, a moment of love.

Nancy Whitelaw